MONSTER HIGH

DIARIES

MONSTER HIGH™
DIARIES

DRACULAURA
AND THE NEW
STEPMOMSTER

By Nessi Monstrata

LITTLE, BROWN AND COMPANY
New York Boston

Little, Brown and Company

Hachette Book Group
1290 Avenue of the Americas, New York, NY 10104
Visit us at lb-kids.com

Little, Brown and Company is a division of Hachette Book Group, Inc.
The Little, Brown name and logo are trademarks of Hachette Book Group, Inc.

The publisher is not responsible for websites (or their content)
that are not owned by the publisher.

First Edition: August 2015

ISBN 978-0-316-30084-1

10 9 8 7 6 5 4 3 2 1

RRD-C

Printed in the United States of America

Diary Entry

You are totes not going to believe this...my dad <u>is getting married!</u> Another vampire caught his eye at the Ice Ball in Antarctica last year. He saw her across the room, asked her to dance, and was sucked in. Just like that! Isn't it the scary-cutest story ever?

I don't think there is anything sweeter than love at first bite.

Dad's trying to play it cool. (You know Father. Always so serious!) But from what he's told me, Ramoanah (that's her name!) is just amazing and he's totes into her. After that night at the ball, they spent the next few months chilling out in Antarctica, and now

THEY ARE GETTING MARRIED!

I ♡ weddings!

But here's my tiny, little, itsy-bitsy secret. (Just a teensy thing. No big deal, I'm sure.) I'm kinda freaking out. I don't actually know much about Ramoanah. Since she and Dad have been away in Antarctica and I've been here—attending Monster High—I haven't even met her. And she's going to be my stepmomster in less than a week!

I'm sure she's going to be fangtastic, just like Dad says she is. How could she not be? Still, I'm a little nervous, you know? What if she...

Ugh! I can't even write it!

What if she...doesn't like me?

I know, I know. That would be silly. We'll probably be beast friends, right? We'll share style tips and watch boo-vies together. Maybe it will be so fangtastic having her around that it will be hard to even remember that it's been just Dad and me for the past 1,600 years.

I can't wait for the wedding—it's going to be so glamorous and elegant! And I'm so excited for my ghoulfriends to see what a real Transylvanian vampire wedding is like. They will all get to learn more about my vampire scaritage. The ghouls can meet my family and a ton of old vamp friends. Here's the best part: We all get to stay at the Chateau Transylvania (it's the fanciest hotel EVER—even Cleo will be impressed!).

Oh, and I have a feeling that I might get to be Ramoanah's maid of horror!! Or at least a batsmaid (that would be totally ghoul too). I'm hoping she will ask me as soon as we meet....I want to be prepared, so I'm going to buy the most fangtastic hot pink and black dress ever created. I was so thrilled when Dad told me that Ramoanah had chosen black and pink as the colors for the wedding—looks like she and I have the same fave colors! I can't wait to help her with all the final wedding plans when we get to Transylvania tomorrow!

Gotta go! More soon.

Smooches,
Draculaura

CHAPTER ONE

hat do you think, ghouls?" A sweet and cheerful vampire named Draculaura stepped out of the changeling room at Neiman Monstrous, her favorite store in the Maul. She spun in circles. A shimmering, lacy black dress with beautiful hot pink details swirled around her legs. The dress matched her black-and-pink-streaked hair perfectly and made her pale pink skin glow. "Is this the one?"

5

"Gore-geous," Clawdeen Wolf proclaimed as she stopped pawing through racks of dresses to check out her ghoulfriend. Clawdeen was a fierce and stylish werewolf with a nose for fashion. "It's perfect."

Frankie Stein's one green and one blue eye went wide. "That pink makes you look totally voltageous, Draculaura." Frankie, the only daughter of Frankenstein, also had a scary-cute style all her own, though she loved just about anything with black-and-white stripes.

"I think we have a winner." Draculaura giggled. Then she slipped behind the curtain to change back into her school clothes. "Don't you just love weddings?" she called as she carefully pulled off the dress. "I can't believe my *dad* is the one getting married!"

"You haven't been to a wedding until you've been to a royal wedding," Cleo de Nile announced. Cleo—a mummy and Egyptian princess who was as loyal of a friend as she was a pampered diva—

was sprawled out on a sofa nearby, impatiently waiting for the glass of fresh-squeezed orange juice she had insisted the shop clerk bring her to sip on while she waited for her friend to choose a dress for Dracula's wedding. "Oh, but I'm sure your dad's wedding will be really great too...."

"It's going to be totally amazing, Draculaura!" Clawdeen agreed excitedly. "I'm stoked that us ghouls all get to come along. I never thought a werewolf like me would be taking *two* trips to Transylvania so close together."

Draculaura stepped out of the changeling room. "I'm excited too, ghouls. I feel so lucky that I get to have my beast ghoulfriends there with me. I just wish everyone at Monster High could come!" She sighed. "Because of course, the one little thing that would make this weekend extra fangulous would be having Clawd along. I'm going to miss my sweetie so much. Going to Dad's wedding without him totally bites."

"No way," Clawdeen replied quickly, shaking one sharp fingernail at her beast friend. The last thing she wanted was one of her siblings tagging along on the trip of this lifetime. Her pack stuck together too much as it was—sometimes, she just wanted to be with her beasties. "This weekend it's just us ghouls. And it's going to be clawesome!"

Their zombie friend, Ghoulia Yelps, grunted her agreement. Ghoulia blinked behind her horn-rimmed glasses and readjusted the headband in her long, thick blue hair. She tucked the book she had been reading into her purse for later.

Cleo rolled her eyes playfully and yawned. "If we ever leave the Maul, that is. Are you almost done, Draculaura? I think I aged another year while we waited for you to pick something."

"Ready!" Draculaura said cheerfully. She knew Cleo was only teasing—after all, Cleo was a stylish mummy who enjoyed shopping as much as any other ghoul!

The Neiman Monstrous clerk—a slow-moving zombie—grunted as she lurched toward the counter to ring up Draculaura's purchase.

"I love that it's just going to be us ghouls too but...I don't get why Clawd *can't* come along," Frankie said.

Draculaura frowned as she replayed in her head the conversation she'd had with her dad. Her father had been acting sort of weird in the days leading up to the wedding. Ever since he'd called to tell Draculaura about his fiancée, he had been acting even more serious than usual. Draculaura was pretty sure it was just prewedding jitters. But she was still a little hurt about what he had said when she asked for permission to invite Clawd. She told her friends, "My dad thought Ramoanah's family might have a hard time swallowing the fact that I'm dating a non-vampire. Vampires, werewolves...you know. We're not exactly known for getting along."

"Well, we'll just have to help change their minds about that!" said Clawdeen.

"I'm sure everything will be fine," Draculaura said quickly. She hoped Clawdeen was right... but deep down she worried that it might not be so easy. "My dad is always super welcoming to other monsters. I'm sure Ramoanah will be too. Her relatives are probably just a little more conservative than Dad and I are. As you ghouls know, some vampires can have a teensy, eensy problem with anyone who isn't a vampire...so I think Dad just wants to play it safe."

"Some old, stuffy vampires like Lord Stoker," sniffed Clawdeen, thinking about her last trip to Transylvania with Draculaura. Lord Stoker had tried to make Draculaura believe she was the long-lost vampire queen. Luckily, Draculaura and her ghoulfriends figured out that Lord Stoker was tricking her, along with the rest of the vampires, so he could continue to control the vampire court. Draculaura and the Monster High crew had managed to find the *real* vampire queen—Draculaura's old friend Elissabat—and made Lord Stoker look like a fool.

"Exactly." Draculaura giggled. "There are still a lot of vampires like Lord Stoker in Transylvania. The kind who think vampires should be the most respected and feared monsters in the world." She rolled her eyes at the silliness of it all.

"Ugh," groaned Cleo. "That is so last century. Besides, it's obvious that if any monsters were to be the most respected in the world, it would be the de Niles." Cleo smiled at her beast friend and asked, "Isn't that right, Ghoulia?"

Ghoulia patted Cleo's arm and smiled. Sometimes, it was easiest just to agree with Cleo. Ghoulia knew her beast friend had pretty strong opinions and really loved when people agreed with her.

As they strolled out of Neiman Monstrous, Frankie said, "I bet the food is going to be totally electric!" She grinned as she imagined the fancy new foods she would get to try. "And speaking of food…Ramoanah's family knows you're a vegetarian, though, right, Draculaura?"

Draculaura cringed. Unlike every other vampire she had ever met, she didn't drink blood—she preferred fruits and veggies and lots of protein supplements. Just the thought of blood made her queasy, and she had been known to faint at the mere mention of the word!

Draculaura and her dad had discussed her vegetarianism a lot over the years—it was hard for her dad to understand how Draculaura could be so different from other vamps. But deep down, she knew Dracula respected her choice. "I don't know if they know…" she said, her voice trailing off uncertainly. "I mean, I'm sure my dad must have told Ramoanah, but I don't know if she told her family or not. I hardly know anything about Ramoanah, actually. The only thing I know for sure is that my dad is batty about her and that she's going to be a part of my family. I'm going to have to spend a lot of time getting to know her before the wedding!" She tried to smile, but her deepest worries about having a new stepmomster were rearing their ugly heads in her mind, and that made it almost impossible to pull off a real smile.

Her ghoulfriends could all sense something was wrong. Ghoulia asked Draculaura what was eating her.

"It's nothing," squeaked Draculaura.

"Come on," prodded Frankie. "You can tell us. We're your beast friends."

Draculaura clutched the dress bag in her arms. She knew that telling her ghoulfriends what she was worried about would probably make her feel much better. "It's just that…even if Ramoanah's great—which I'm sure she will be!—I'm sort of nervous about everything changing."

"I get it," said Clawdeen. "It's been just you and your dad together for the past sixteen hundred years. It's definitely going to be different having a stepmomster around."

"But it's going to be great," added Frankie.

"You think?" asked Draculaura. "I just don't know how we're going to fit someone new into our family after all this time. And what if my dad likes her more than he likes me? Or what if Ramoanah doesn't like me? What if things change, and…"

"Things will change. That's unlife," Cleo said firmly. "But the other stuff you're worrying about is totally ridiculous," she added in a softer voice. She placed a hand on Draculaura's shoulder to comfort her. "Your dad loves you. That's never going to change."

The other girls nodded. Ghoulia said, "Everyone adores you, Draculaura. You're such a true ghoulfriend."*

---

* *Translated from Zombese*

"Ghoulia's right," said Clawdeen. "Everyone loves you. And your dad has room for both of you in his life. Ramoanah is going to adore you too."

Frankie hugged her friend. "No one could ever take your place in your dad's heart."

"Thanks, ghouls," Draculaura said with a smile. "You're the beast." After talking through her concerns with her ghoulfriends, she certainly felt much better. They were right. She was probably worrying for no reason.

They had a fangtastic wedding weekend to look forward to. She wasn't going to waste a moment of it worrying. She grinned and linked arms with her ghoulfriends. "We leave tomorrow, so you know what that means—just a few hours to find the perfect wedding shoes!"

And just like that, all of Draculaura's worries about meeting Ramoanah floated away as she and her ghouls hunted for the most perfectly fangtastic shoes in the Maul.

Diary Entry

<u>I *LOVE* Monster High</u> to the max, *BUT* there is something so exciting about visiting Transylvania. I just love getting to reconnect with my vampire scaritage. It brings back so many <u>fangulous memories</u> of growing up in the vampire court. Sometimes it feels like forever ago that Dad and I fled Transylvania for the Boo World.

Just between you and me, it was hard for me to leave Transylvania. I missed my friends, the pretty mountains, and all that lovely purplish night sky. It sure did help that Dad had our whole house rebuilt in the Boo World. So even though unlife is super different now than it was when we lived in Transylvania, the Boo World feels like home.

And of course, I've met so many creeperific monsters at Monster High that I can't even imagine going back to the old life. I would never have met Frankie, and Clawdeen, and Cleo, and Ghoulia, and Lagoona, and CLAWD, and...well, you get my point.

Sometimes I forget that Frankie hasn't seen much of the world yet. She was totes adorable when we boarded the train for Transylvania today. She got so electrified about the trip that she began to spark, and all the lights in the train went out! That poor ghoul...she just can't help but get excited about new adventures.

And speaking of being excited, my sweet little pet bat, Count Fabulous, is going batty too! He loves the Boo World, but I can tell he is happy we are going back to Transylvania!

Well, gotta fly! More later.

Smooches,
Draculaura

CHAPTER TWO

This way please, ladies." A tall vampire in a three-piece suit greeted Draculaura and her friends at the train station. "I am Fangsly, one of the Chateau's senior butlers. I have been tasked with your care for the weekend. We have a carriage waiting for you over here that will take you to the Chateau."

"Ooh, a butler!" Clawdeen said, wiggling her eyebrows. "For us?"

"Now, that's more like it," Cleo said. "My luggage is over there, Fangsly. I expect it will be delivered to my room at the Chateau first thing."

"As you wish, miss," Fangsly said, bowing. "Miss Draculaura, welcome home. Your father has asked me to deliver you to the hotel immediately so that you will all have time to freshen up in your suite before the bride's family gala this evening."

"Gala?" asked Frankie.

"Yes, miss," confirmed the butler. "Tonight the bride's family is hosting a welcome dinner for the esteemed guests of Dracula and Lady Ramoanah. A prewedding welcome party, so to speak. Dinner, dancing, and a reception."

"This is all so fancy!" Draculaura said, climbing into an elegant carriage. Heavy velvet curtains were draped over the windows. She pushed them open so her friends could get a better view of her homeland as they drove up the mountain to the

Chateau. "Do you think Ramoanah's family did all of this to welcome us home to Transylvania? I feel like royalty!"

Cleo took a deep breath and settled into the plush cushions inside the carriage. "Draculaura—I must say, I'm impressed with Transylvania's hospitality. They sure know how to make a princess feel at home here."

When they arrived at the hotel, a small crowd was gathered just outside the big oak front doors. "What is that about?"* groaned Ghoulia.

"I don't know what's happening," Draculaura answered, peeking out from behind the curtains. Fangsly whisked open the door of the carriage for them and began unloading their luggage. The ghouls hopped out and made their way toward the growing crowd.

"What's going on?" Frankie asked someone near the back.

---

* *Translated from Zombese*

"Look, it's Elissabat!" a cheerful young vampire squealed. "Our queen!"

The young vampire's friend added, "Also known as the greatest boo-vie star of all time—Veronica von Vamp! She's signing autographs."

"Ooh!" exclaimed Draculaura, standing on tiptoes to try to see over the crowd. "Elissabat is here? I didn't know she was going to be here for the wedding!" She waved her arms in the air. "Elissabat—over here!"

The crowd that had gathered near the Chateau's grand entrance all turned and stared. Someone nearby whispered, "Isn't that Draculaura...? She's the vampire who found Elissabat and persuaded her to come home to lead us as our queen!"

"Draculaura!" Elissabat said, rushing over to greet her old friend. "It's so fangulous to see you again. I was very happy to receive an invitation to your father's wedding. It has been years since I last saw him!"

Draculaura gave her vampire pal a hug, then stepped back so her ghoulfriends could greet Elissabat as well.

Suddenly, a camera crew swooped in and surrounded the group. Cleo smiled radiantly and put her hand on her hip. "Make sure you get my good side!" She began posing, then nudged Draculaura and whispered, "I realize the cameras are probably here with Elissabat…but there's no harm in letting them know that another royal is here too!"

Draculaura couldn't help but giggle at Cleo's antics, even as she squinted in the bright camera lights.

Elissabat snapped her fingers and waved the cameras away. "That's a wrap for now. Please give us some time to say hello before you start filming!"

"Don't be silly," Cleo said, still posing. "I'm happy to let them film me at any time. I know how much people love to see footage of royalty, and I love to give the people what they want."

The crew packed up their cameras and walked away. Cleo called after them, "I'll be here all weekend. You're free to point those cameras in my direction at any time!"

"I'm glad the cameras don't bother you," Elissabat said. "They're with me all the time lately. You see, after I became the vampire queen, my studio decided to do a reality show about my unlife as both queen and Hauntlywood actress. When they heard I'd gotten an invitation to Dracula's wedding, they thought this would be the perfect opportunity to get some great shots of the vampires of Transylvania at their very best. So we're doing a piece on vampire scaritage and what it means to celebrate a marriage, vampire-style. I told them I would allow them to film things this weekend as long as the cameras don't get in the way of the festivities!"

Cleo laughed. "How could cameras ever be in the way? And I'm sure they're going to be thrilled to have footage of me too. Look at us!" She linked arms with Elissabat. "A vampire queen and an Egyptian princess. Hauntlywood will be dying of excitement. Transylvania is bursting with celebrity and royalty this weekend!"

One of Elissabat's assistants whispered something in her ear. The vampire queen nodded. She said, "I'll see you tonight at the bride's family gala, ghouls. But now, duty calls." Elissabat and her entourage walked off, followed by the crowds of screaming fans.

"This weekend is going to be totally voltageous!" Frankie said to Draculaura as they made their way into the Chateau's enormous lobby. "A spooktacular wedding, a Hauntlywood boo-vie crew, you get to meet your new stepmomster—"

"Oh my ra!" Cleo said, interrupting her. "Look at this place. You were right, Draculaura—this hotel really is fit for a queen."

The lobby of the Chateau Transylvania was indeed a sight to behold. The giant space was filled with dark purple candles that appeared to be floating in midair. The walls were covered in thick black tapestries with elaborate ruby red designs woven through them. The floors were made of black marble that gleamed in the candlelight. Vampire butlers stood hunched in every corner, ready to serve.

"Allow me to show you to your room." Fangsly suddenly appeared out of nowhere and gestured for the group to follow him.

"Can you just wait for a sec?" Draculaura asked. She looked around the lobby, disappointed to find it mostly empty. "I was just hoping to say hello to my dad before we go upstairs."

"Ooh!" said Frankie. "And maybe we can meet Ramoanah. We need to thank her for inviting us to the party tonight!"

"I'm afraid your father is unavailable at the moment," Fangsly said coolly. "He has stepped out, with plans to return before this evening's gala reception."

Ghoulia grunted. "He is probably just seeing to last-minute details."*

Draculaura reluctantly nodded. "You're right, Ghoulia. I'm sure he has a ton of wedding stuff to take care of." She gave her friends the brightest smile she could. "I guess I'd just hoped that Ramoanah and my dad would be here waiting and that I could spend some time with them before the rest of the guests fly in. I wanted to offer my help and see if they need me to do anything for the wedding. I want to see Ramoanah's dress too. But I guess I can wait until tonight!"

"You'll have plenty of time to get to know Ramoanah over the next few centuries or so," Frankie reminded her with a smile.

"You don't have to spend every second with your new stepmomster this weekend," Clawdeen

---

* *Translated from Zombese*

teased as the five of them linked arms and followed Fangsly through the hotel's dim passageways. "For now, you can kick back in a clawesome suite with your four ghoulfriends. Let's get ready to knock 'em dead with our killer style tonight! I, for one, have the perfect outfit to wear for dancing the night away!"

Diary Entry

My dad and Ramoanah are obviously
trying so hard to make all my ghoulfriends
feel so very welcome in Transylvania! I am
surer than ever that Ramoanah is going to be
fangtastic! Sending that special carriage to
pick us up, our very own _BUTLER_!!, and
this fangulous suite. (Half of Monster High
would fit inside this hotel room with us....
It's seriously that huge!) Uugh-mazing.

Dad's open-mindedness about other
monsters is one of the things I love most
about him. He's worked so hard to fight for

the rights of all monsters around the world—
and he's always been really great about
accepting all my non-vamp friends. A lot of
important vampires are so old-fashioned,
and Dad gets that traditions can change. I bet
Ramoanah is just as open-minded!

Ooh! Gotta go. Frankie just found another
room in our suite, and I'd better check it out.

Smooches,
Draculaura

CHAPTER
THREE

This room is a scream come true!" Frankie cheered when Fangsly propped open the door to their huge hotel suite.

"Oh my ra!" Cleo said, stepping inside the cavernous room. "Now this is a suite fit for a princess!"

"Whoa!" exclaimed Clawdeen. "Clawesome." Beside her, Ghoulia's and Draculaura's mouths hung open in wonder.

"I take it this is to your liking?" Fangsly stood still as stone near the door while they raced into the suite. Much like the Chateau's lobby, their room was dimly lit and totally elegant. Right inside the door of the suite was a huge sitting room filled with comfortable chairs and couches and a huge chaise longue.

Off the sitting room were five bedrooms, each with its own bathroom! Cleo quickly claimed the room with a plush canopy bed. Clawdeen took the smallest room, which was filled with gold-tinted faux-fur rugs that made the space feel warm and cozy. Ghoulia immediately settled into a bedroom that was lined in bookshelves filled with all kinds of books. Frankie snagged the room that was wallpapered in black-and-white stripes.

"Just look at this coffin!" Draculaura squealed, running into the last bedroom. In the center of the room, there was an enormous coffin lined in dark pink silk. The room was stuffed with beautiful black and pink roses. Count Fabulous flapped into the room and got cozy in one corner of the pink ceiling. "Thank you, Fangsly. This room is so totes freaky fab."

"Make yourselves comfortable," the serious butler said. "The bride's family has asked me to inform guests that dinner will be served at eight o'clock in the Scaritage Ballroom. They have requested that everyone arrive promptly. Dancing will follow the formal dinner."

"You got it," said Clawdeen. "Turn on some music, and these ghouls will be there!"

Fangsly added, "If there is anything you need this weekend, just ring for me and I'll fly up straightaway."

Draculaura and her ghoulfriends flounced from room to room in their suite, checking out all the secret nooks and comfy corners in each bedroom. Then they gathered in the sitting room to get dressed for that night's reception. The ghouls tried on several different outfits, giggling as they each held a mini fashion show in the center of their very own Chateau Transylvania suite.

Cleo looked royally gore-geous in a dress made of gold and teal bandages with gold snake-strap sandals and a scarab necklace. Ghoulia was fiercely elegant in a bright red shredded taffeta minidress. Frankie looked voltageous in a sleek neck-to-knees black-and-white lightning-bolt-print dress. Clawdeen's sparkling purple tiger-print dress was offset with a gold studded belt and a pair of killer black-and-gold boots. And Draculaura was wearing a fangtastic layered, ruffled pink skirt with a black glitter top with pink lace trim and a jeweled pink bat-wing necklace.

When they had all brushed and wrapped and primped (and charged up, in Frankie's case), they made their way back down to the lobby to explore the hotel for a bit before the dinner was to begin.

"Draculaura!" someone called from near the door. "Yoo-hoo! Draculaura, dear."

"Ooh!" Draculaura said, tugging her friends toward a group of glamorous-looking vampires. She whispered, "Come and meet Lady and Lord Coffington. They're like an aunt and uncle to me. They took care of me sometimes when Dad and I were still in the vampire court."

"Draculaura," Lady Coffington said, her arms out in a welcoming gesture. "It's lovely to see you, my dear." She glanced at Draculaura's friends and lowered her arms. "And who are these...creatures?"

"These are my ghoulfriends from Monster High, Lady and Lord Coffington. This is Cleo de Nile, Frankie Stein, Ghoulia Yelps, and Clawdeen Wolf."

Lady and Lord Coffington exchanged a look. "I thought you would have become friends with"—Lord Coffington cleared his throat—"the other *vampires* at Monster High."

Draculaura giggled. "Don't be so old-fashioned, Lord Coffington," she teased, holding out a finger and playfully wagging it at him.

Lord Coffington took a deep breath and finally forced a smile. "I've been undead a good long time, young lady. It can be hard to change your ways after hundreds of years." Reluctantly, he nodded at Draculaura's friends and said, "Please accept my apologies. Of course any friend of our dear friend Draculaura is a friend of ours. Welcome to Transylvania."

Lady Coffington nodded and smiled awkwardly at Draculaura's friends, then leaned in to Draculaura to whisper, "Has Lady Ramoanah met your ghoul-friends yet, dear?"

Draculaura shook her head. "No. I haven't even met her yet!"

"Well," said Lady Coffington, her smile grow-ing even more strained. "That should be...inter-esting."

Suddenly, the front doors of the Chateau were flung open, and a large group of vampires clad in fang-to-toe black swept into the lobby. In the center of the crowd—tall, handsome, and impossible to miss—was Dracula.

"Father!" Draculaura cried, rushing over to greet him.

"Draculaura," Dracula replied, pulling his daughter close for a hug.

Draculaura stepped back and looked at the other vampires who had come into the Chateau with her father. They all stared back at her, unblinking. They were so still, so serious-looking, that it almost seemed as though they weren't even real. Their skin glowed white in the candlelight that lit up the lobby, and dark circles surrounded their gleaming black eyes. *This must be Ramoanah's family*, Draculaura thought. Draculaura's gaze settled on a frighteningly beautiful woman who was right next to her father. In a timid voice, she said, "You must be Ramoanah?"

The woman nodded, lifted one perfect eyebrow, and said, "How do you do?"

"I'm Draculaura," Draculaura said excitedly. "It's so fangtastic to finally meet you." Draculaura looked expectantly at her new stepmomster-to-be, hoping she would pull her in for a hug or at least crack a warm smile, but instead Ramoanah just stood there looking rather stiff and uncomfortable. *Maybe she'll need a little bit of time to warm up...?* Draculaura thought uncertainly.

"It's an honor to finally meet you," Ramoanah said without moving.

"Draculaura," her dad said, touching Ramoanah's arm. He glanced between his daughter and his wife-to-be. "Darling, we have a few finishing touches to put on the welcome gala that Ramoanah's family is hosting tonight. We also have several last-minute wedding details to attend to. If you'll excuse us, I'm sure you and I will have a chance to catch up later. As Fangsly has probably already told you, all our honored wedding guests will be gathering in the Scaritage Ballroom very shortly."

"Oh," murmured Draculaura. "Um, okay. I guess I'll just see you at dinner tonight, then." She glanced at Ramoanah and her family and smiled warmly despite her disappointment. "Thanks for inviting us to the welcome gala. I bet it's gonna be fangulous."

"We have invited *all* the guests who have already arrived in Transylvania for the wedding," a woman standing beside Ramoanah said in a harsh voice. She introduced herself as Ramoanah's mother. Her hair was streaked with gray, and she wore a chilly frown on her face. "Your father told us you were arriving today, and it seemed…inappropriate to not extend an invitation to you and your…guests. Despite our hesitation."

"Hesitation?" asked Draculaura.

"Mother…" Ramoanah said in a low voice.

Dracula quickly spoke up. "Ramoanah's family was originally thinking of having a *small* dinner party with only a few members of their immediate family. But when we realized how many of our guests would have already arrived—including Elissabat and Lord and Lady Coffington and, of course, you—Ramoanah and I suggested that they include everyone. That's why we have a bit of a last-minute scramble to make sure the kitchen is ready for our larger party."

"Why don't you help your dad and Ramoanah with some of the last-minute stuff?" Clawdeen suggested.

"Yeah, Draculaura. You're great at planning parties," agreed Frankie enthusiastically.

When Draculaura's two friends spoke, the crowd of vampires around her father swiveled their heads to gape at them. Draculaura tried to ignore their stares and hoped her ghouls would do the same.

"Right!" Draculaura said cheerfully. "My ghoulfriends and I would love to help with absolutely everything this weekend. Ramoanah, I would be honored to help you with your dress or makeup or..." Her voice trailed off as she noticed how uncomfortable Ramoanah looked and how angry Ramoanah's mother looked. After a long moment of silence, she continued in a tiny voice. "Or, you know, anything else you might need?"

"I'm quite sure I can...manage things just fine," Ramoanah replied.

"Fine with me," Cleo sniffed. She didn't like the chilly tone these vampires were taking with Draculaura. Besides, she had no intention of lifting a finger this weekend. That's what servants were for after all.

"Draculaura," said her father gently. He looked apologetic. "Many members of Ramoanah's family have just arrived at the Chateau. They still need to check in to their rooms and dress for dinner." He gestured to the vampires standing around them. "As the hosts of tonight's gala, Ramoanah and her family would—ah—*prefer* to handle the preparations on their own."

"Without my help?" Draculaura asked sadly.

"That is correct," announced Ramoanah's mother. "We do not *need* nor *want* help from any of—"

Draculaura cringed as she waited for Ramoanah's mother to finish what she was saying, but Clawdeen cut her off. "Let me guess. You don't want any help from non-vampires, am I right?"

Instead of replying, Ramoanah's mother sniffed and turned her head.

"Perhaps we should go check on things in the kitchen," Ramoanah suggested a moment later. "Mother, would you please go check on things in the dining room?"

Without another word, Ramoanah's mother swept off toward the dining room as Ramoanah took Dracula's hand and gently pulled him toward the kitchen. Dracula managed a small smile at Draculaura and her friends as he was whisked away.

"Let me know if you change your mind and decide you need anything," Draculaura called after them. "Anything at all…" But neither Dracula nor Ramoanah turned around.

"Well," Frankie said a moment later. "That was, um…interesting?"

Draculaura was close to tears. "That was a major fail! So much for my hope that I'd get to be her maid of horror. I'm surprised she even invited me to the wedding!"

"She did seem a bit chilly," agreed Clawdeen. "Maybe she spent a few too many months in Antarctica," she joked, trying to make her beast ghoulfriend smile.

Draculaura sighed. "What am I going to do? My new stepmomster hates me!"

"She doesn't hate you," Frankie said, and all the ghouls nodded in agreement.

"How could she hate you?" Clawdeen added. "She only just met you! And besides, you happen to be absolutely fangulous, remember?"

Draculaura couldn't help but smile.

"Give her some time. She is probably as nervous as you are,"* moaned Ghoulia.

"You're right, Ghoulia," said Draculaura, perking up even more as she saw the encouraging smiles on the faces of her friends. "Maybe I do need to just give her some time to warm up to me. I'll kill her with kindness, and soon she won't be able to resist me!" She beamed at her friends. "It's going to be fine, right?"

"That sounds more like the ghoul we all know and adore," Cleo said. She put her arm around Draculaura's shoulders. "Now, who wants to explore this golden Chateau before dinner?"

* *Translated from Zombese*

44

Diary Entry

I know Dad must have told Ramoanah that the ghouls from Monster High would be here for the wedding. It was Dad who told me they could all come in the first place (he's also the one who told me Clawd couldn't come along), so I can't understand why Ramoanah's family acted so chilly toward all of us.

As for Ramoanah's chilliness...well, I'm going to look on the bright side (as I always do!) and assume that Ramoanah just has prewedding nerves or something. Maybe she was so busy with wedding stuff that she forgot to mention it to her family. And that's probably what's making her seem a little unfriendly. I'm sure she must be nice when you get to know her a little better, or Dad wouldn't have fallen in love with her. Right? He said she was sweet, so I guess I'll just have to wait to see that side of her for myself.

I can't wait for the welcome gala. It will be so nice to get to sit and chat with Ramoanah and Dad during dinner. We can talk all about the wedding, and I'm sure they'll decide to let me help out with some of the last-minute plans.

I bet the food at the Chateau Transylvania is <u>to die for!</u> And dancing!! Clawdeen and Frankie are so excited there's going to be dancing. I wonder if they'll play the theme song from the new Vampire Majesty boo-vie? Wouldn't it be a scream to see Elissabat dancing along to a song from the boo-vie she starred in?! Oh, and maybe we can teach everyone the zombie shake! How fangtastic would that be?!

Gotta go explore the Chateau before dinner. More later.

Smooches,
Draculaura

CHAPTER FOUR

The ghoulfriends had such a blast exploring the west wing of the Chateau that they lost track of time. "We're going to be late for dinner if we don't hurry!" Draculaura squeaked.

In their hurry to arrive on time for dinner, they got lost as they wound back toward the lobby through the twisting corridors. There were dozens of hidden passageways in the Chateau, which dated back thousands of years. Every time they came around a corner, they stumbled upon a new and fangtastic room they hadn't seen before. There was an art gallery in the east wing of the Chateau, alongside an elegant gift shop and a jewelry store that sold precious ancient gems. (The ghouls had to drag Cleo out of there, and she only agreed to leave after Draculaura promised her there would be plenty of time later for shopping!) The west wing of the Chateau housed a super-fancy spa that the ghouls agreed they couldn't wait to check out later in the weekend.

When they finally got to the Scaritage Ballroom on the second floor of the Chateau, dozens of vampires were already seated at tables that filled the room. The room was buzzing with conversation and laughter, but when Draculaura and her ghoulfriends stepped through the door, a hush fell over one whole side of the room. Draculaura gazed at the faces staring up at her from the silent tables and could see that there were many vampires she didn't know. The rest of Ramoanah's family, she guessed.

"Darling," said Dracula, sweeping over to greet Draculaura. He looked at his pocket watch and frowned.

"I'm sorry we're a few minutes late," Draculaura said quickly.

"Not at all, not at all," Dracula assured her. "Dinner will begin in just a moment. Please, take your seats quickly."

"Where are we sitting?" she asked, linking arms with her father. "I'm so excited we finally have some time together! I want to talk to Ramoanah about her dress and the song she picked for your first dance and the cake and—"

"Draculaura." Dracula cleared his throat. "I'm, ah—I'm seated with Ramoanah's family tonight. They have set up a table for you and your friends over there." He pointed to a table on the opposite side of the room. "We put you next to Elissabat and her Hauntlywood people! I know how much you've missed your childhood fiend—you must have so much to get caught up on. So Ramoanah, uh…*we* thought you might like to sit near her at dinner."

Draculaura tried to hide her disappointment. It seemed like she was never going to get to spend any time with her dad! She couldn't help but feel as if her father and Ramoanah were trying to keep her away from the rest of the wedding party. Is this what it was going to be like for the rest of her unlife? Would Ramoanah always push her to the side?

She tried to swallow, but a lump caught in her throat. Draculaura forced a smile and said, "Do you think Ramoanah has a moment before dinner begins? I would love to greet her, since she's the host of the gala." She searched the faces in the room, looking for her new stepmomster.

"Or maybe I should greet her parents first? I guess they're the official hosts of tonight's dinner?"

"Well, yes," said Dracula. "They are the hosts. But there's really no need to greet them right now."

Draculaura couldn't believe her ears! "I remember my manners, Dad. You taught me well! You always told me it's important to greet the host immediately upon arrival."

Dracula smiled slightly. "Perhaps you can do that later. Why don't we see how the evening goes first, yes?" He turned to wave hello to another guest, adding, "I'll find you after dinner, darling. It's best that you find your seats now so the dinner service can begin. We want to have plenty of time for dancing later."

As they made their way through the tables full of wedding guests, Draculaura stopped to say hello to everyone she knew. The ballroom was filled with vampire friends and relatives she hadn't seen in centuries. She introduced Cleo,

Ghoulia, Frankie, and Clawdeen to her aunt Scabitha, her uncle Bury, and their son, Dragos.

"A pleasure to meet you," Dragos said smoothly, standing up and bowing to Draculaura's ghoulfriends.

Frankie giggled when Dragos took her hand in his and kissed it. "A delight to meet you," Dragos murmured.

"Same here," said Frankie. Dragos dropped her hand quickly when a bolt of electricity shocked him. Frankie put her hand over her mouth and said, "Oops, sorry about that."

Frankie leaned toward Draculaura and whispered, "He's so *electrifying!*"

They paused to greet another table full of old fiends Draculaura had played with when she and her dad had lived in the vampire court. She was so excited to introduce her ghoulfriends to everyone!

When they finally got to their table in the farthest corner of the room, Draculaura happily greeted one of her oldest ghoulfriends—and the vampire queen—Elissabat, and waved hello to the Hauntlywood crew. The vampire queen required an extralarge table in order to fit her whole camera crew and all the various Hauntlywood assistants who helped keep her makeup, hair, and wardrobe just right. Clawdeen immediately began chatting with Viperine Gorgon, Elissabat's personal makeup artist. The two had met during the ghouls' first trip to Hauntlywood, and they couldn't wait to get caught up on everything that had happened since!

The reality show cameramen were spread around the room, capturing every elegant moment. The whole scene felt like something out of a boo-vie. Draculaura couldn't believe that her father's wedding would be part of a reality television show!

"Helloooooo," cooed Cleo, gesturing to one of Elissabat's cameramen. "I see the cameras are ready.

Please, feel free to film me at any time this week-end. Perhaps one of the crews should be assigned to *me*?" She batted her eyes and smiled her most dazzling smile. "Now that the cameras are everywhere, I'll make sure I'm ready for my close-up at a moment's notice!"

"Uh…" The head cameraman looked over at Elissabat, who gave him a small smile and nodded. He turned back to Cleo and said, "Okay, sure. We'll get some B-roll footage."

"B-roll?" squealed Cleo, jumping to her feet. "Do you know who I am?"

"Cleo," Clawdeen said under her breath. "You need to sit down. Everyone's looking at you. And not in a good way."

Cleo looked over at Ramoanah's family. They were all glaring at her in a most unfriendly way. Cleo flounced back in her chair and waved off the cameraman. "We can do my scenes later. That's a wrap for now, boys."

"Whatever you say..." the cameraman replied, rolling his eyes.

A moment later, a team of waiters surrounded the ghouls' table. Dinner was served! As one, they gently placed covered platters in front of each person at the table. Then, on an unspoken count of three, they whisked the gleaming silver lids off each person's plate.

"Oh..." moaned Draculaura, just before her eyes fluttered closed and she slumped against the back of her chair.

"Oh no!" Frankie cried, grabbing Draculaura's arm before she completely fainted and crumpled all the way to the floor.

Clawdeen stared at the plates that filled the table. Balanced perfectly in the center of each one of the plates was an elegant silver bowl. Inside each bowl was a vampire delicacy—blood pudding. No wonder poor Draculaura had fainted!

Frankie and Clawdeen set to work trying to rouse Draculaura. Elissabat stood up and came around the table to help them. "This used to happen all the time when we were younger," she told Frankie. "Draculaura was never a big fan of the vampire diet. When we used to go to dinner parties in the vampire court, I always snuck in a bottle of tomato juice so she could fake her way through fancy events without telling any of the old-fashioned vampires about her special diet."

"That's so scary-sweet," said Frankie.

"Ghoulfriends watch out for each other," she said, winking. "I didn't want her to go hungry."

Draculaura moaned, and her eyes fluttered open again. Elissabat pushed the bowl away before Draculaura could get another view of her blood-red dinner. "Feeling better, ghoulfriend?" she asked with a smile.

"Bats! I am so sorry!" Draculaura said, embarrassed. She glanced around quickly, checking to see who had seen her faint at the sight of blood. Luckily, it seemed like her dad and Ramoanah were so caught up in conversation at their own table that they hadn't noticed.

Ghoulia and Cleo each pushed their own dinner aside and exchanged grossed-out looks. "Excuse me?" Cleo said to one of the waiters. "Do you have any other options? A fresh fruit plate, perhaps?"

Ghoulia asked if they had any brain puffs hidden anywhere in the kitchen.

One of the waiters shook his head. "No, miss."

"I suppose we'll just go hungry, then." Cleo sighed. "We can order room service later, ghouls." She waved her hand at the waiters and said, "Take it away at once!"

The waiters stepped forward in unison and replaced the covers on each of the ghoulfriends' plates. Then they lifted them off the table, held them high in the air, and glided back to the kitchen.

"Is there a problem here?" a cool voice asked from behind Draculaura's chair.

Draculaura turned. It was Ramoanah. She did not look happy. "Oh, um...hi, Ramoanah. It's lovely to see you again," Draculaura said cheerfully. "Nope, everything's just fine. It's just... well, I'm not sure if my dad mentioned that I'm, uh...a vegetarian?"

Ramoanah took a deep breath. "He did not," she said.

"Well," Draculaura said lightly. "I am! No big deal, though."

Ramoanah pressed her lips together. "It is a big deal," she said in a tight voice. She turned to the other ghouls and asked, "And I suppose none of you are happy with tonight's meal either?"

None of them said anything. After a long silence, Clawdeen finally muttered, "We weren't very hungry. There was a lot of great food on the train. So no biggie."

"No…biggie," repeated Ramoanah slowly, arching her eyebrow. "I would have to disagree. This is unacceptable!" With that, Ramoanah turned and walked swiftly back to her own table.

Did she just call my ghouls and me unacceptable? Draculaura wondered in disbelief. She looked around the table at the faces of her ghoulfriends and could tell they were wondering the same thing.

Draculaura bit her lip. The day that had started out so well was rotting fast. It looked like all her greatest fears about having a new stepmomster were going to come true.

Diary Entry

This dinner is the worst. I snuck back up to the room for a tiny sec, since I need a few minutes to think. I just do not understand why Ramoanah and her family are being so mean to my beast ghoulfriends—and to me!

Even though Ramoanah's family gala is a monstrous fail, I'm not ready to give up just yet. I'm not going to change who I am to make her like me, of course. I can only hope that Ramoanah will come to love my freaky flaws eventually! And anyway, I know we must have something in common, but what that thing is...hmmm. Well, we both like my dad. That's something, at least, right?

Oh! And here's one of the things that makes me think she must be fangulous on some level—her outfit! You should see her **fangtastic dress**! When I first saw her at the gala tonight, it looked like she was just wearing a simple black gown. But when she moved, I could see that it was lined with sparkly pink fur. I think it's a sign—I always trust a ghoul who loves pink! At least we have fashion in common. Of course, it would be nice if we actually liked each other too... you can't build a relationship on clothes alone.

Okay, well, I guess I'd better get back to the Scaritage Ballroom. Dancing is supposed to start soon, and I don't want to miss that!

Smooches,
Draculaura

CHAPTER FIVE

fter the appetizer plates were cleared, the rest of
the dinner service felt like it moved as quickly
as a zombie track race. Course after course was
brought out—and not one of the platters included
foods the ghouls were interested in eating.

Draculaura's head was spinning as she tried to
figure out what was going on with Ramoanah
and her family. They couldn't hate her before they
had even gotten to know her, could they? She
distracted herself from her worries by laughing

with Elissabat. She was laughing nonstop as Elissabat told the other ghouls stories from their childhood.

As the dessert plates were cleared, guests began to stand up and mingle. A string quartet played quiet music in the corner, and the Hauntlywood camera crew continued to wander around the ballroom capturing footage of the evening. Cleo trailed after them, stepping into the center of each shot— ensuring she would be one of the stars of the show. Eventually, she returned to the table when it was clear they weren't very interested in her.

"This is going to be one seriously boring show Elissabat's crew is putting together," Clawdeen whispered to Cleo, yawning. "Are all vampire *galas* so much fun?"

"When they told us we had been invited to a party, I expected a party," Cleo said, perching on the edge of her chair. "I hope the dancing starts soon. This is a total snoozefest. I'm even growing tired of the cameras."

As if on cue, a curtain at the far end of the room flew open, revealing an enormous live orchestra. The conductor lifted her arms, and the strings began to play a slow-moving, formal waltz.

Frankie's eyes nearly popped out of her head as she stared at the instruments and listened to the old-fashioned music. "What is this?"

"Oh my ghoul. They don't expect us to waltz or something, do they?" Clawdeen asked. Her mouth hung open as she watched Ramoanah's large family sweep onto the dance floor in pairs. The dancing couples all glided easily around the dance floor, swaying and spinning in harmony.

"What's next? The Gargoyle Polka?" joked Cleo.

"Come on, ghouls. This is totes fangtastic!" Draculaura said, jumping to her feet. "So maybe a waltz isn't exactly what we had in mind when they said there would be dancing tonight. But let's make the most of it. Remember, I grew up in the vampire court. I can teach you all how to waltz like total pros!"

Clawdeen shrugged. "I guess dancing is dancing. Let's do it." She smiled and pulled Draculaura toward the dance floor.

Cleo saw that the Hauntlywood cameras were now set up along the edge of the dance floor, capturing footage of the dancing couples. So she made her way toward the dance floor and grinned at them. "I suppose a little old-fashioned dancing could be fun."

Ghoulia and Frankie trailed after them. Soon all five of the Monster High ghouls were having a blast on the dance floor. Elissabat and Viperine and the rest of the Hauntlywood crew joined them. Ramoanah's family danced stiffly around the edges of the dance floor, while Draculaura and her ghoulfriends rocked right in the center.

As they twirled and waltzed, Draculaura realized she was having a great time—despite the horrible dinner and less-than-perfect introduction to her new stepmomster. "So maybe this isn't the kind of dancing we're *used to*," she said to Clawdeen and Ghoulia with a smile. "But you all came along to really experience Transylvania, right? This is totally old-school Transylvania! Let's make the most of it!"

The rest of the night was a fangulous blur of dancing and laughing. Elissabat and Draculaura could remember *almost* everything they had learned about the waltz hundreds of years ago. They both turned out to be incredible teachers. Hours later, everyone was danced out and exhausted— and officially starving.

Most of the partygoers had already retired to their rooms to get some sleep. After scanning the ballroom to see if Ramoanah or her father were still there (they weren't), Draculaura suggested they head back to their suite too. "I'll have to thank them in the morning," she said with a yawn. "This was so much fun, but I have *got* to order some room service before I hit the coffin!"

Clawdeen nodded in agreement. "I'm so hungry I would *almost* be willing to eat that—wait a minute, no, still gross."

They made their way through the lobby, then up the dimly lit back stairs that led to their suite. As they were coming around a corner, Clawdeen stopped suddenly and put her finger to her lips. "Shhh."

"I am hungry enough to eat the Monster High Creepateria special,"* muttered Ghoulia.

"I know, I'm hungry too," Clawdeen replied in a hushed tone. "But I just heard someone whispering Draculaura's name."

---

* *Translated from Zombese*

"I'm not sure it's a good idea to eavesdrop," Frankie said, looking to Draculaura to see if she agreed.

"If someone's talking about our friend, we have a right to know what he or she is saying," Clawdeen insisted. "Just listen." The ghouls all stopped. Clawdeen's ears pricked up, trying to catch a snippet of the whispered conversation around the corner.

"I don't want her to find out about..." said a voice. "...know you disagree..."

"That sounds like Ramoanah!" Frankie whispered urgently, her eyes wide.

Another voice piped up. "It's absolutely ridiculous!" Whoever it was sounded angry. "How can Draculaura...?"

"And that's her mom!" noted Cleo. "What are they talking about?"

"Shh," Clawdeen growled. "Quiet, so I can hear."

Ramoanah mumbled something more, then said more loudly, "Enough! I won't stand for it!"

"You must, Ramoanah," hissed the other voice. "We are *vampires*. It's tradition."

Ramoanah muttered something more, but even Clawdeen's extrasensitive ears couldn't pick out any specific words.

"What's she saying?" Cleo asked.

"Shhhh," urged Draculaura. She couldn't imagine how awful it would be if they were *caught* eavesdropping on Ramoanah! It was revolting enough that they were talking about her.

There was the sound of a door opening, then Ramoanah said, "...will just have to deal with it!" A door slammed, and the conversation was over, just like that.

Draculaura and her ghoulfriends were left alone in the hall again. "What was that all about?" Draculaura wondered aloud. "Find out about what? Deal with what?"

No one had any answers. But it sure didn't sound good.

Diary Entry

I can't stop thinking about the conversation we overheard on our way back to the suite last night. It sure sounded like Ramoanah and her mother were fighting about me! I don't know what I did to make her dislike me so much, but it's pretty clear we're not going to be instant beasties. Boo.

Also, one of the things Ramoanah said last night is really bugging me. I can't stop thinking about how she said she didn't want me to find out about something. <u>What</u>?! What was she talking about?

Does Ramoanah have some secret she's keeping from me? Is it possible she's also keeping secrets from my dad? Dad is all about honesty and openness...if Ramoanah is hiding anything, shouldn't he know about it before he commits to her for eternity?

What am I supposed to do????? :(

Smooches (and yawns),

Draculaura

CHAPTER SIX

The next morning, the ghouls all slept in to recover from their late night of dancing. Fangsly delivered a small room-service breakfast order shortly after they woke. When he opened the door, he apologized for how few non-vampire food options the hotel had on hand—just a small pitcher of tomato juice and some cereal he had managed to scare up. The ghouls had already discovered that the hotel's evening menu wasn't much better—they had found it nearly impossible to find anything on the room-service menu the night before. They were all starving!

Fangsly promised that the manager was working on improving the menu. "Unfortunately, we weren't able to greatly improve the food selections before breakfast." Fangsly bowed, long and low. "We didn't realize that we would have so many distinguished guests at the Chateau this weekend with unusual food needs."

"It's not your fault, Fangsly," Draculaura said, taking the tray from him with a smile. "Don't worry about it. We're not going to starve."

"Oh, but I must worry," Fangsly said seriously as he stepped back into the hall. "The hotel has been given an order. We must do everything in our power to make your kind feel welcome for the rest of this weekend."

"An order?" Clawdeen asked. "An order from who?"

Fangsly shook his head. "I am not at liberty to say who. This person says the only thing that matters is the comfort of our guests, especially those staying in this suite."

"O-*kay*," Frankie said, shutting the door.

"Well, at least it's nice to know someone's looking out for us," Cleo sniffed. "Probably Elissabat. I'm sure her boo-vie crew is as hungry as we are!"

While they ate, they chatted about Ramoanah. Everyone wondered what kind of secret she was hiding and worried over what Ramoanah and her mother had been arguing about. "They probably think I'm rude for not eating the food they served at their welcome gala!" Draculaura groaned. "Her family was nice enough to invite me to this nice dinner, and I fainted!"

"Don't be silly," said Cleo. "If it were really a welcome gala, they should have made everyone feel welcome by giving us food we could eat." She relaxed back on the chaise longue. "You know what's going to get your mind to stop worrying about your stepmomster? A spa day!"

"Ooh," Frankie cheered. "The spa in the Chateau looked totally creeperific. What do you think, Draculaura? Can we take you down there for some primping? Maybe a prewedding manicure will help you feel better."

Draculaura took the last sip of her tomato juice and nodded. "You're right. I have to stop worrying about everything, or I'm going to make myself crazy. A spa day would be totes amazing!"

As the ghouls got ready to head down to the Chateau's fancy spa, Draculaura had an idea. "Call me batty, but what do you think about my inviting Ramoanah to join us at the spa? Maybe a ghouls' day is just what we need."

"I think that's a great idea," Frankie said. "You can suggest it to her and see how it goes."

Draculaura rang for Fangsly, who was back at their door in a flash. "Fangsly, do you happen to know where my dad and Ramoanah are this morning?"

"Yes, miss," he said.

"I'd like to invite Ramoanah to join us at the spa," she said.

"Of course," Fangsly said with a bow. "Would you like me to extend the invitation on your behalf?"

Draculaura giggled. "Don't be silly, Fangsly! I want to invite her myself. Can you show me where she is? I'd look for her myself, but this place is huge, and I'm sure I'd be lost in no time."

Fangsly bowed again. "Certainly. Please, follow me."

Draculaura's spirits soared as she pictured the look on Ramoanah's face when she invited her for some stepmomster-daughter bonding. She was still sure that if she and Ramoanah spent a day together, talking and relaxing, they would become fast fiends. As she left the suite, she called back, "Ghouls, you can go ahead. I'll find Ramo-anah, and hopefully we'll both meet you at the spa in a few!"

"Are you sure you want to do this alone?" Frankie asked. "I'm happy to come with you for moral support."

"Oh, don't worry, I'll be fine." Draculaura smiled widely. "This is my new stepmomster we're talking about. Go ahead. Pick a scary-cute color for my toes, okay?"

The others headed toward the spa as Fangsly led Draculaura through the lobby and into the Chateau's elegant dining room. "Oh," Draculaura said quietly, looking around. "I'm not interrupt-ing her breakfast, am I?"

"Not at all," Fangsly promised. "They have just finished."

"They?" Draculaura wondered aloud. She wasn't in the mood to see Ramoanah's family again, but she steeled herself for the possibility. It was very unlikely Ramoanah would be eating breakfast in the restaurant alone.

Fangsly led Draculaura all the way through the restaurant. At the back of the dining room, he pushed aside a large velvet curtain and opened a rich mahogany door that led to a private dining room.

When they stepped through the door, Draculaura stopped. Inside, Dracula, Ramoanah, Ramoanah's family, and many of Draculaura's oldest family fiends were enjoying breakfast together at a long table in the center of the room. "Oh," Draculaura said, waving meekly. "Hi, everybody." She swallowed and said quietly, "I didn't know we were all meeting for breakfast!"

At first, no one said anything. After a long, awkward silence (during which Elissabat shot Draculaura an apologetic half smile), Ramoanah said, "We thought you would rather not join us for breakfast." She focused her gaze on Draculaura.

"After last night's…ah, *mix-up* at dinner, we didn't want to put you in an uncomfortable position again. The menu at the hotel restaurant is not *vegetarian* friendly."

"Do vegetarians even eat breakfast?" Ramoanah's mother muttered under her breath.

"Of course we eat breakfast!" Draculaura said, trying to keep her voice light. She was working hard to keep the hurt out of her voice but was finding it difficult. They had all met for a family breakfast…and no one had invited her! It was almost impossible to not feel left out. She felt tears prick at her eyes, and her throat felt tight.

"I didn't want to interrupt your morning with your friends," Dracula said suddenly, standing up. "I assumed you would be spending the day with them."

"I—" Draculaura began.

But before anything more could be said, Ramoanah stood up. "Let's forget breakfast for now, shall we? Draculaura, I'm glad you've come by, actually."

Really? Draculaura wondered, brightening.

Ramoanah continued. "I wanted to introduce you to my dear nephew, Alexander."

A tall, handsome, and extremely unfriendly-looking vampire dabbed the edges of his mouth with his napkin and stood up. "Ah," Alexander said, sizing up Draculaura. "So I finally meet Dracula's famous daughter. Charmed, I'm sure."

"Nice to meet you," she said, stepping forward to shake hands.

"Aunt Ramoanah has told me that apparently..." Alexander cleared his throat and stuffed his hands into his pockets. "I have been given the *chore* of escorting you down the aisle at the wedding ceremony tomorrow. I will be your wedding date, so to speak." He said the word *date* like it was something rotten.

"Oh?" Draculaura said. She wasn't sure how to respond. Was it her imagination, or was Alexander being frightfully rude? She didn't want to turn down his invitation, but it was pretty clear he wasn't very excited about the prospect of being her date. "Um...I'm not sure what you mean. I have my ghoulfriends here. We will all be going to the wedding together...."

Dracula smiled and said, "I'm sorry we haven't told you yet, dear. But Ramoanah would like you to be her maid of horror." He looked from his wife-to-be to his daughter.

Ramoanah gave her mother a quick look, then nodded.

"For real?" Draculaura squealed. "I would *love* that! Thank you! What do you need me to do? Would you like me to help you get ready before the wedding tomorrow? I can help you get dressed! Or help with flowers or..." Ramoanah managed a small smile, and Draculaura felt her heart swell with joy. Maybe she was finally breaking through Ramoanah's shell! "Anything. Just name it, and I'm your ghoul!"

"There is not much left to be done," Ramoanah said, glancing again at her mom. Ramoanah's mom cleared her throat loudly and scowled, and Draculaura was instantly transported back to the whispered conversation from the night before. The joy she had felt just moments earlier drifted away as she saw the look that passed between Ramoanah and her mother. She wondered—once again—what Ramoanah and her mother had been arguing about. Was Ramoanah being forced to ask Draculaura to be her maid of horror because it was a tradition? Did Ramoanah not really want her to be her maid of horror after all?

Draculaura kicked the thought out of her mind. She had to stay positive! "Okay, well, just let me know! And it's great to meet you, Alexander. We'll have a blast at the wedding tomorrow."

Alexander looked down his nose at Draculaura. "I think not."

Draculaura pretended she hadn't heard him. But as the waiters swept into the room to clear the breakfast plates, she figured now was as good a time as any to suggest Ramoanah join her and her friends at the spa. "Ramoanah, I know you must have so much to do to get ready for the wedding, but...if you can spare an hour, my ghoulfriends and I wanted to invite you to join us at the Chateau's spa. Maybe we could get matching nails for the wedding tomorrow?"

For a brief moment, Draculaura thought Ramoanah was going to accept her invitation, but then the moment was gone and Ramoanah shook her head. "I'm afraid I must say no. I have other commitments."

"Okay," squeaked Draculaura. She suddenly felt foolish for even having asked. "No problem."

"We have so many last-minute details, and Ramoanah wants to spend as much time with her family as she can before she moves with us to the Boo World," added Dracula with a tight smile. "You understand, don't you, dear?"

"Yes," Draculaura said quietly, stepping backward. "Of course." She blinked back tears. Her dad and her stepmomster had so many last-minute things to get ready for the wedding but no need for her help. She got it. "Well, if you change your mind, you know where I'll be." With a final wave at the others, she turned and ran out of the Chateau's dining room.

Draculaura hustled to the spa, quietly fuming. Even the lavender scent wafting out of the spa wasn't enough to calm her. She had moved from thrilled to hurt to fangry in a matter of moments.

Her friends were all bundled in soft plush robes, sipping mineral water, and relaxing in the spa's comfortable lounge. "What happened?" Frankie said, jumping up as soon as she saw the look on Draculaura's face.

"She said no," Draculaura said, her mouth set in a grim line. "To my spa invitation, to my offer of help getting ready for the wedding, to everything. But she did ask me to be her maid of horror."

"She did?" Frankie cheered. "That's great!"

"Not great, actually." Draculaura moaned. "I think she felt like she had to. It's tradition. A vampire bride is always supposed to ask the closest female family member to be her maid of horror. It would have been really strange if she *hadn't*. If my dad or Ramoanah had a sister, she could have avoided asking me, but since they don't…I'm the only other possibility. Obviously, Ramoanah's family is all about tradition. I'm sure her mom must have told her she *had* to ask me." Her eyes were bright with tears. "I would be excited if I thought she had *wanted* me to stand beside her at the wedding. But I really don't think that's how it is."

Frankie and Clawdeen held up a soft robe, urging Draculaura to slip into it. Meanwhile, Ghoulia pushed Draculaura's feet into a pair of comfortable slippers. When the Hauntlywood crew came into the spa, their cameras at the ready, Cleo waved them away. She knew that the last thing Draculaura wanted was for Hauntlywood to capture her family drama on film!

Draculaura slumped down in a chair and hung her head in her hands. "Ramoanah and her family obviously have a problem with who I am."

As her friends listened, Draculaura explained how horrible she had felt when she realized she hadn't been invited to the family breakfast. And then all her feelings of frustration bubbled up to the surface. "I'm going to feel like a stranger at my own dad's wedding!" she exclaimed sadly. "It's obvious Ramoanah hates that I'm a vegetarian, she's been mean to all of you, and she and her mom are keeping some kind of secret—probably about me." She looked up and finally shared her deepest, darkest fear. "They're probably trying to figure out how to keep me away from my dad forever. What if she's trying to get Dad to move back to Transylvania with her? What am I going to do?"

The ghouls weren't sure what to tell Draculaura (the situation did seem every bit as gloomy as Draculaura feared it was), so they did the one thing they could do—be supportive of her.

"Her family is just a bunch of stuffy old grumps," Clawdeen announced.

"She doesn't deserve you as a stepdaughter, Draculaura," Cleo added.

"You've done everything you can do to try to get to know her," Frankie said soothingly. "You tried your beast."

"So what am I supposed to do?" Draculaura asked again. "It's not like she and I can avoid each other for the rest of our lives—even though that's probably what she wishes would happen." She sighed heavily. "I guess once I'm back at Monster High, she can just pretend I don't even exist. Soon, my dad will forget all about me—"

Ghoulia cut her off, shaking her head and muttering, "You are his only daughter. That will not happen."*

"I know that he won't *really* forget about me, Ghoulia," Draculaura said, flopping back into the comfortable spa chair. "But it's pretty obvious that unlife as I knew it is totally going to change. Gone is the open-minded Dracula who embraces all kinds of monsters and welcomes different ways of thinking. From here on out, it's going to be all old-ghoul vampire everything. What if she *does* make us move back to Transylvania?!"

As the ghouls soaked their toes in tubs filled with hot, fizzy water brought in from the

---

* *Translated from Zombese*

Transylvanian foothills, they tried to figure things out together.

"Is anyone else dying to know what Ramoanah doesn't want Draculaura to find out about?" Clawdeen said quietly. "What is it she's hiding?"

Ghoulia looked thoughtful. "If you really want to know, you will have to ask Ramoanah herself or express your suspicions to your father."*

"Those are my only two options?" Draculaura said. "Confront Ramoanah directly or talk to Dad about it?"

"Ghoulia's got a point," Frankie said. "I think it's time for you to talk to your dad. After all, if she *is* hiding something from your dad, he needs to know that there's a secret. And he needs to know how bad you feel about the way Ramoanah's been treating you."

"So you think I should talk to him?" Draculaura

---

* *Translated from Zombese*

asked. "Do I tell him I think she's keeping some sort of secret? Won't it seem like I'm tattling?"

"I don't think you have much of a choice," Cleo said. The other ghouls nodded in agreement.

Before she could lose her nerve, Draculaura set off to find her dad. If his new wife was keeping something from him, he deserved to know.

Diary Entry

Part of me hopes that Father will tell me
I'm wrong about everything. But even I
know that's batty.

What if Ramoanah convinces my dad that
our way of unlife is wrong? What if spending
time with all these traditional vampires makes
Dad think that the old way of unlife is better
than our new way?

What if—gulp—he makes me _leave_ Monster
High?!

I wish _Clawd were here_—but then again, I
guess I don't. Because if Ramoanah doesn't

like my ghoulfriends, what would she think about Clawd?! She'd probably make me break up with him, and that would just break my heart.

The ghouls and I are trying to make the most of Ramoanah's traditional vampire wedding celebrations. We even danced the waltz! Why can't she see that some parts of the Boo World can be *fun* too? If only there were some way to combine Ramoanah's family's stuffy traditions and some of the Boo World traditions, this wedding would be killer. A traditional vampire wedding with a Boo World twist...that would make Elissabat's Hauntlywood people scream with excitement!

It would be SO FANGTASTIC.

Oh well. I'm not a part of planning this wedding, so I guess there's no point in thinking about it. Time to talk to Father.

Smooches (and wish me luck!),
Draculaura

CHAPTER SEVEN

Draculaura left her ghoulfriends at the spa and hunted Fangsly down at his usual perch in the lobby of the Chateau. "Hello, Fangsly," she said. "Have you seen my father? I need to speak with him."

"Yes," Fangsly said, turning on his heel. "He is in the study. Please, follow me."

Draculaura did as she was told, following him past a wine cellar and a centuries-old library and through an enormous cave filled with sleeping bats. "This is our employee break room," Fangsly explained. "Some of us like to squeeze in a little bat nap between shifts."

Past the cave, he pushed open a door and led Draculaura into a room that looked almost exactly like the study Dracula had in their castle back home.

"You look comfy," Draculaura said to her father as she sank into one of the leather chairs facing the desk. "Settling in here in Transylvania?"

"Yes," Dracula said, putting down his pen. "This hotel goes to great pains to ensure its guests feel at home while they're staying at the Chateau."

"They do. Unless you're a vegetarian or a non-vampire and you want to eat something other than blood," Draculaura said quietly.

"Darling..." Dracula sighed. "Ramoanah and I are terribly sorry about last night's meal. In all the excitement, I simply forgot to tell the kitchen we would need to provide choices for our non-traditional guests."

"You forgot?" Draculaura said. "You *forgot* I'm a vegetarian? And you *forgot* that I—and Elissabat, our vampire queen!—would be bringing along some of our non-vampire fiends?"

"I forgot to mention that you were a vegetarian," Dracula replied. "I forgot that I had never told Ramoanah about it," he added. "And yes, I simply forgot to think about the needs of our non-vampire fiends. I am very sorry." His gaze met Draculaura's. "Ramoanah was so embarrassed."

"She was?" Draculaura said, narrowing her eyes.

"She was. And other than that one oversight, I hope that you and your friends have felt comfortable the rest of the weekend," Dracula said. "We have gone to great lengths to welcome your friends to Transylvania in true vampire style."

"Yeah," Draculaura agreed reluctantly. "Everything has been really lovely. It's just…"

Dracula waited. After a long moment, he said, "Just?"

"It's just that I get the feeling Ramoanah and her family don't like me very much," Draculaura whispered.

Draculaura waited for her dad to disagree, to tell her she was crazy for even thinking such a silly thing. But he didn't. He sat, stroking his chin. Finally, he said, "Ramoanah's family is very traditional."

"You think?" Draculaura said, rolling her eyes.

Her dad chuckled. "They come from a long line of conservative vampires who have spent many years believing that their way is the right way." Draculaura began to cut in, but her father put up a hand to stop her. "I know you may be thinking that makes this relationship between Ramoanah and me a strange one. A less-than-perfect match. But away from her family, Ramoanah is very different. She understands my mission in the Boo World, even if it is not the path she would have chosen for herself. At the beginning of our relationship, after falling in love at first bite, we did not see eye to eye. And there are still many times when she finds it hard to swallow our way of life. But she is coming around. She is warming up slowly. Though we may not agree on everything, we do have great respect and love for each other."

"Let's hope it doesn't take three hundred years for her to warm up to me."

"You know, Draculaura, that our family is different from many of our kind. Just as we have come to embrace and understand other monster cultures, we must also learn to appreciate some traditional vampire customs. Ramoanah's family has different beliefs, and I hope that you will respect them for who they are."

"Of course I will," Draculaura promised. "But I think it's only fair that you tell her she has to do the same with me! She hasn't even *tried* to get to know me!"

Dracula closed his eyes. A familiar, playful smile appeared on his face, and Draculaura was pleased to see a bit of the father she was used to at home. "You are very outgoing, Draculaura. It's one of the things I most admire about you. You're welcoming and generous with your friendship, and you always have a positive outlook on life. Your way of looking at the world does not come as easily to some people."

"Are you telling me Ramoanah is shy...or just mean?"

Her dad smiled. "Shy, yes. And though she is not *mean*, as you put it, it can be hard to crack her exterior. But when you do...well, I can tell you it's well worth the effort it takes to get to know her." His smile grew wider.

"Okay, okay!" Draculaura laughed. "I don't need to hear you get all gooey about your fiancée." She took a deep breath, then said, "Dad, is everything going to change?"

He nodded. "Much will change, yes. It's just been the two of us for many years, dear. And I treasure that time we've had together, as father and daughter. But we have room for others in our lives. Think of how much your world expanded when you met your friends at Monster High. There is an endless supply of love in our hearts—they grow and change as we welcome new people into our world."

Dracula reached across the desk and took his daughter's hand in his own. "We will not lose the life we had before, after I am married. The next sixteen hundred years will be even better—because with Ramoanah in our family, we will develop new traditions. She will introduce us to many new things that will improve us in ways we can't imagine."

Draculaura wasn't so sure about that...but what she *was* sure about was how much her dad obviously loved his bride-to-be. The look on his face told her everything she needed to know: Her dad was in love.

Even though a life with Ramoanah as her step-momster still worried her, Draculaura knew she couldn't possibly squash her father's happiness by sharing more of her fears. Whatever secret Ramoanah was hiding, whatever she thought about Draculaura, didn't matter. Her dad deserved love. She would just have to figure out how to make it work.

Draculaura was grateful that her dad had made her feel better about her biggest worry: He wouldn't stop loving her just because he loved Ramoanah. He had a space for both of them, and, hopefully, Ramoanah would eventually find a place for Draculaura in her heart too. Draculaura was determined to never give up hope that some-day, Ramoanah would come around. She hoped that eventually—one, ten, or a thousand years from now—she and Ramoanah would figure out how to be friends.

"I assure you, Ramoanah cares about you more than you realize," Dracula said. "She is trying."

"Thanks, Dad." Draculaura stood and blew her father a kiss. "I guess it helps to hear you say that. And you know I'm happy for you, right?"

"I do," he said with a smile. "You are such a sweet ghoul. I'm proud to call you my daughter."

Draculaura left her father's borrowed study feeling better than she had before. She hurried back to the suite to tell the other ghouls all about her conversation with her dad. But when she got there, she found it empty. There was a huge fruit basket with a note attached. Draculaura's stomach rumbled at the sight of all the delicious, juicy fruit. She took a bite out of an apple and opened the note. It said:

Enjoy your lunch. Someone had the most voltageous food delivered to our room! Can you believe it? There was an enormous steak for Clawdeen (she devoured it in about two bites), a huge bag of fast food for Ghoulia, a tray of kebabs for Cleo (plus a bushel of grapes for dessert and even a butler to feed them to her!), and a WHOLE CHEESE SCREECHZA for me!

Back soon!
—Frankie

"Frankie?" Draculaura called out, wandering from room to room. "Clawdeen?"

She checked every wing of their suite and found them all empty. Only Count Fabulous remained, perched high up in the corner of her coffin room.

Puzzled, she rang for Fangsly. "Yes, Miss Draculaura?" the butler said, appearing at the door of their suite just moments later.

"Did you bring us all this delicious food?" she asked. "You're too sweet! Do you want to share some fruit with me?"

"The food was not from me, miss," Fangsly replied. "And no, thank you. I prefer my food to be...bloodier."

"Oh," Draculaura said, wrinkling her nose. "If you didn't send it up, who left all our favorite foods for us, then?"

"I am not at liberty to say." Fangsly shook his head.

"Come on, Fangsly. You can tell me—I thought we were getting to be fiends!"

Fangsly's lip curled up in something resembling a smile. "I'm sorry, miss. But I do hope the snack is to your liking."

"It's delicious!" Draculaura sighed and bit into a juicy peach. "The other thing I'm wondering is, have you seen my ghoulfriends?"

"I have."

"Great!" Draculaura said. "Where are they?"

"They left the hotel a short while ago, Miss Draculaura. Lady Ramoanah ordered a carriage for them." He looked apologetic when he said, "Your friends are gone."

Diary Entry

Gone?

Where ARE they?!

Fangsly refuses to tell me anything more, and, believe me, I asked him about a hundred times.

What if Ramoanah put my ghoulfriends on the train back to Monster High? She wouldn't have done that, would she?

I called Dad, and he told me to stop overreacting. He says he doesn't know where they are either, but he told me I don't need to get so worked up about it.

Worked up about it?! Hmmmm, why would I worry? Let's see: My soon-to-be stepmomster, who doesn't like my ghoulfriends or me, just put my beasties in a carriage and sent them off somewhere on the day before her fancy, traditional vampire wedding. I think it's fair that I'm _freaking out_ just a little bit, don't you, Diary?!

Okay, I'm gonna go enjoy this fangtastic fruit basket that someone sent up for us and play with Count Fabulous. Making him look adorable always _makes me feel better._

Smooches,
Draculaura

CHAPTER
EIGHT

The afternoon dragged on. Hours later, there was still no sign of any of Draculaura's ghoulfriends at the Chateau.

Draculaura killed time by dressing her pet bat in every single outfit she had packed for him—his cute little tuxedo, a frilly satin suit, and the soft pink fur cape with matching earmuffs. But even playing dress-up with Count Fabulous didn't make her feel much better. She couldn't stop worrying about where Ramoanah had sent her fiends.

After the fruit basket was gone and Count Fabulous had escaped to his perch in the corner of her room, Draculaura wandered down to the lobby. She bumped into Elissabat and her crew, who persuaded her to sit for an on-camera interview with one of the Hauntlywood producers. Viperine worked her makeup magic and made sure Draculaura looked perfect before they asked her any questions, and they had a whole bunch of snacks for her to munch on while she was waiting for them to get the lights set up. They asked her a ton of fun questions about Monster High and her fiends, and they wanted her to describe her perfect wedding. It was actually sort of fun (though she could only imagine how upset Cleo would be when she found out she'd missed her chance to shine).

When she'd finished her interview, she and Elissabat went for a walk on the Chateau grounds. The sun was setting behind the mountains, and

Draculaura got to soak in some of the beautiful views she missed from her childhood. When the last of the afternoon light was shining behind the mountains, it almost made them look like they were glowing purple and silver.

As she and Elissabat returned to the lobby after their walk, they bumped into Alexander. He was with Ramoanah's mom. "Hello again," Draculaura said cheerfully.

Alexander smiled formally at Elissabat, but when he looked at Draculaura, his lips curled into the same sneer she had seen at breakfast earlier. Draculaura couldn't help herself—she turned away and rolled her eyes. He was just so snobbish! Luckily, Alexander didn't notice. Instead, he said to Draculaura, "Got rid of the filth, did you?"

"What are you talking about?" she asked.

Alexander laughed and drawled, "That wolf and all the other nasty creatures you dragged along to Transylvania, of course." He nodded at

Elissabat, adding, "Our extraordinary vampire queen is much more appropriate company for you."

"You can't talk about my ghoulfriends like that!" Draculaura exclaimed. Alexander just laughed.

Elissabat stepped forward and hissed, "You are totally out of line."

"Defending the trash, then, are you?" sneered Alexander, speaking quietly. Surely, he knew he was being very disrespectful!

"Draculaura and her ghoulfriends are better monsters than you'll *ever* be, Alexander. You should feel lucky you have the honor of walking down the aisle beside her tomorrow. She can show you something about being a good person."

Alexander laughed coldly. "Walk beside her? I think not. As soon as I realized how much time *she*"—he flicked his eyes toward Draculaura—"spends with *freaks*, I told my aunt I didn't want to be paired with her at the wedding tomorrow. Ramoanah knows that if she wants me to be a part of the wedding, she will need to find someone other than Draculaura to be her maid of horror. I refuse."

Draculaura sucked in her breath. Elissabat pulled her arm. "Ignore him," she said, tugging her into the lobby.

"He's horrible!" Draculaura gasped through tears. "The whole family—they're all awful. Every last one of them!"

"They're not used to your way of unlife," Elissabat pointed out. "In many ways, you are better off than Ramoanah's family. You acknowledge that there's a world outside Transylvania. Most vampires do not. Still, you must remember that your way of unlife is very different from theirs. Many of our kind do not understand why the Boo World is appealing. But they will come around. In time."

She smiled. "At least, I hope they will. That is something I'm working on now that I'm the leader of this world. You have a head start, Draculaura. Vampires are slow to change. But eventually, everyone will have to come around. Vampires can't ignore the Boo World forever. This is my duty as the queen."

Before they could discuss it further, the lobby doors flew open. Cleo, Clawdeen, Frankie, and Ghoulia burst into the lobby. They were all laughing. "Where have you—" Draculaura began. But her words caught in her throat when she saw that Ramoanah was lingering in the doorway behind them. "Been?" she squeaked.

Ramoanah pulled her cape over her face, spun, and turned into a bat. She flew off into the night air before Draculaura even had a chance to say hello.

Cleo shrugged, her lips curling into a secretive smile. "We had a little project."

"What kind of project?" Draculaura prodded.

Clawdeen and Frankie exchanged a look. "Ramoanah had something she wanted our help with." Frankie giggled.

Draculaura gaped at them. Ramoanah wanted *their* help? She had refused all of Draculaura's offers, but now she was including her ghoulfriends in the wedding preparations? How strange. What did Ramoanah have hiding under her wings?

Ghoulia leaned toward Draculaura and muttered, "Ramoanah is actually quite engaging."*

"It's true," Frankie agreed. "She's not as bad as we thought. I think she might be coming around."

"Well, ghouls, this day is a wrap," Cleo said suddenly, yawning. "We have *got* to get our beauty rest for tomorrow. This wedding is going to be epic."

As she followed her ghoulfriends to their room and watched everyone get ready for bed,

---

* *Translated from Zombese*

Draculaura realized she was now more confused than ever. Not one of the ghouls would tell her anything about where they had been all day or why Ramoanah had wanted their help. Draculaura knew she should be happy that her stepmomster had—apparently—been kind to her beast ghoulfriends, but instead, she just felt left out. Again. As she drifted off to sleep, there was only one thing Draculaura felt sure of: Weddings rot.

Diary Entry

Today's **the day**.

    I can't believe how excited (and yes, a little nervous too) I was for Dad and Ramoanah's wedding just a few days ago. Now, with only a few hours left until I get a new stepmomster, I couldn't be any less excited.

    When my fiends got back to the Chateau with Ramoanah last night (where _WERE_ they??), I felt so left out. Maybe Dad's right—maybe Ramoanah is trying to be more accepting of our way of life. But why would she invite my ghoulfriends to help her with wedding stuff when there is nothing I want more than to help too?!

Is it just me? Is it possible that Ramoanah just doesn't like me?

Honestly, I don't even know if she still wants me to be her <u>maid of horror</u>. When Alexander told me he wasn't going to walk down the aisle with me, it definitely bit. He and I were supposed to be partners, but I guess I'm on my own. Or maybe Ramoanah found someone else to be her maid of horror so she wouldn't have to lose Alexander in the wedding party. I'll find out soon enough.

I would give <u>**anything**</u> to have Clawd here with me.

Sigh. How am I supposed to enjoy the wedding when I'm feeling so worried and hurt about everything that's happened since we arrived? Weddings are supposed to be happy...but at the moment, I'm feeling anything but.

Smooches, even though I'm
not even in the mood ☹,
Draculaura

CHAPTER NINE

While all the ghouls got ready for the wedding the next day, Draculaura tried her hardest to act like everything was okay. She helped Frankie with her dress, found the perfect new necklace for Cleo in the Chateau's jewelry store, and styled Clawdeen's hair in the most amazing updo. But deep down, she was feeling rotten.

The wedding was to be held at a castle near the Chateau. Late in the afternoon, the ghouls piled into an enormous carriage that would take them—along with Elissabat, some of Draculaura's closest family fiends, and the Hauntlywood crew—from the Chateau to the ceremony. All the way there, everyone laughed and chatted and *ooh*ed over the views of the mountains. Everyone, that is, except Draculaura. She just sat and stared out the curtained window, worrying. She tried to act like everything was normal whenever the Hauntlywood cameras were on her, but even that was difficult.

That morning, she had received word from Fangsly that she was supposed to join the rest of the wedding party in the castle dungeons before the ceremony. There, she would wait with the bride, groom, and wedding party until the public ceremony began. In vampire custom, the bride and groom always spent the moments before their vows together, celebrating privately with their families before standing before the rest of the guests.

As the carriage bumped over the drawbridge in front of the three-thousand-year-old castle, Draculaura could see that the grounds had been decorated so beautifully that it almost felt as if they were stepping into a fairy tale. She took in a deep breath, wishing she really were stepping into a fairy tale...one with a happy ending.

When they stepped out of the carriage, she kissed her ghoulfriends on their cheeks and told them she'd find them after the wedding.

"Good luck," Clawdeen called after her, a mischievous smile playing at her lips.

"Say hi for us!" Frankie giggled, waving.

Draculaura waved back. Inside, her dad greeted her at the bottom of the stone steps. They linked arms, and he led her to the cavernous dungeons, where Ramoanah's parents and family were already gathered. The damp stone walls glowed with pink lights, making the space seem almost cheerful.

Draculaura had to admit that everything in the castle was very glamorous and beautiful—it felt like the kind of place where she would like to have her wedding some day.

But unlike today's wedding, *her* wedding—to Clawd, of course!—would be filled with all kinds of people from many different parts of her life and many different backgrounds.

"How are you today, dear?" Dracula asked as they walked together through the tunnels under the castle. This was the last time she and her dad would be together as a family of two—after this, there would be three of them.

"I'm happy for you, Dad," Draculaura answered honestly, giving him a hug. Though she wasn't happy about starting off on such a rotten note for her life with Ramoanah, she knew that this day wasn't about her. Her dad was happy, and so she could find a way to survive—for him.

"Draculaura." Ramoanah stepped forward when she and her father reached the dungeons. Draculaura couldn't believe how fangulous Ramoanah looked in her sleek black wedding gown with soft pink lace trim and an elaborate, swirling pink train. She might not be very nice, but she certainly was stunningly gore-geous. Ramoanah lifted one arm and gave Draculaura an awkward half hug. It was the warmest greeting she'd given her all weekend. "Thank you for being an important part of our day."

"Of course, I wouldn't miss it," Draculaura said, hugging her back. She wasn't sure how important she had been. She'd done nothing more than show up and bring in a bunch of Boo World friends, which had apparently not gone over very well. But at least Ramoanah was finally trying to be nice. "You look beautiful, Ramoanah," Draculaura said honestly.

Ramoanah accepted the compliment with a small smile. "I believe Alexander has already told you that he would rather not be a part of the wedding today?"

"He did," Draculaura said, her stomach tight. "I'm sorry I messed things up for everyone."

Ramoanah considered her for a long moment. "You need not apologize. In fact, it is I who should apologize. I'm sorry our relationship has gotten off to a difficult start."

"Really?!" Draculaura exclaimed. "That means so much to me, you have no idea!"

"I hope you don't think that I've been *trying* to be unwelcoming," Ramoanah said, taking her arm. "I believe your father has already explained that my family is very different from yours."

Draculaura nodded. "I guess I'm a little different from most vampires you know, huh?"

"Yes, you certainly are," Ramoanah said. "I tried

to prepare my family for what was to come, but I'm not quite sure they realized just *how* different you are from the usual ghouls we spend time with. I will admit that even *I* was not entirely prepared to meet you. As you know, your dad"—Ramoanah glanced at Dracula—"forgot to tell me you are a vegetarian! I was horrified when I realized we had not provided the right kind of food for you at our welcome gala. If I had realized, I would have made certain we had something special prepared for you. I was so uncomfortable about that oversight!"

"I thought you were mad at me for not eating your fancy dinner that night!" Draculaura said. "I was so worried I was being rude."

"I certainly was not mad," Ramoanah replied. "Embarrassed, yes. Did you enjoy the special treats I had delivered for you and your friends yesterday afternoon?"

"*You* sent us all that delicious food?" Draculaura asked. "We were wondering who had sent that for us! It was perfect!"

"I hope that helped to make up for the welcome gala and for the breakfast we couldn't invite you to be a part of. I had words with the hotel after the welcome gala, asking them to expand their dining menu for our less-than-traditional guests." Ramoanah leaned in close and lowered her voice to a whisper. "Please know that I am working on my family too—hopefully, in time, our families will find a way to understand and respect one another."

"I hope so too."

"Now, as for Alexander and his rude choice to exclude himself from the wedding..." Ramoanah smiled widely as her voice trailed off. She was looking at someone over Draculaura's shoulder. "I've found you an alternate date. I hope you will find him suitable?"

Draculaura turned—and came face-to-face with Clawd! "Clawd," she screamed, rushing into her boyfriend's arms. "What are you doing here?"

"Ramoanah invited me," Clawd said, bending down so Draculaura could scratch his ears. "She booked me a first-class ticket on the train to Transylvania, and here I am!"

"After the food disaster at the welcome gala, I wanted to find some way to make it up to you. Though my mother does not approve of my decision, I decided that inviting Clawd to join us for the wedding would be the best way to show you that I support your lifestyle in the Boo World." Ramoanah nodded at Clawd, then said to Draculaura, "You live a very different life than I'm used to, but I want you to know that I am ready to be a part of it. I'm proud of the work your dad does. When I agreed to marry him, I knew it would mean a big change. I hope you can show me how to embrace change,

Draculaura—after seeing you make the most of our waltz at the gala, I realized you are obviously very good at making the most of new situations!"

Draculaura cuddled against Clawd and brushed a tear from her eye. "I would love to help you. I think you're going to *love* the Boo World when you see how much fun we have!" Her head was swimming as she tried to take all of it in. Then a thought popped into her head. "So, where did you go with my ghoulfriends yesterday?"

"Ah, yes," Ramoanah said, smiling. "I wanted to make sure the wedding reception would be inclusive of all the guests—not just vampires— but I needed some help with that, and I thought your friends would be the best ones to go to for advice. I hope you will love all the things we came up with to make this a wedding celebration that everyone can enjoy!"

"I can't wait," Draculaura said happily. "If my friends were involved, I bet it's going to be fang-tastic!" She stepped out of Clawd's arms long enough to wrap one arm around her dad and another around her new stepmomster. "But first, who's ready to say 'I do'?!"

Diary Entry

That was the _most amazing wedding_ ever!
Everything was so beautiful—Ramoanah's
dress, the beautiful black roses, fireflies and
pink silk everywhere, my sweetie in a tux!!!
And the food—oh my ghoul, the food.
Yesterday, I guess my ghoulfriends gave
Ramoanah a ton of suggestions for delicious
bites she could serve to non-vampires, and
she ordered _everything_! We ate like queens
in the castle—macagroany and cheese bites,
boo-cumber salad, chocolate-and-strawberry
fon-boo, a sculpture of the Transylvanian

mountains made out of FRUIT. It was amazing.

One of the best parts of the whole wedding was the music! My super brilliant ghoulfriends suggested that Ramoanah let some of Elissabat's Hauntlywood people plan the wedding sound track. Instead of boring old waltzes all night—the usual vampire wedding tradition—they totally mixed things up. Even Ramoanah joined us on the dance floor with Elissabat when the theme song from the new Vampire Majesty boo-vie played. And Frankie went electric when my cousin Dragos invited her to dance!

(Even though snobby Alexander refused to come out and dance with everyone, I could totes tell he wanted to. Maybe someday he'll come around. Then he'll realize how much he's missing out on in the Boo World!)

This has been a wedding weekend I won't forget! But I guess I'd better go pull Cleo away from the Hauntlywood cameras. We've got to get on the next train back to Monster High. It's been fun visiting Transylvania, but I think I've spent enough time with traditional vampires this weekend to last another unlifetime. Well, at least until we have to have the holidays with Ramoanah's family...that should be, um, interesting?

Here's what I've discovered this weekend: Maybe Ramoanah isn't exactly warm and fuzzy (like my Clawd!), but I think she and I are going to get along just fine once we get to know each other better. It's definitely going to be fangulous having a stepmomster around—maybe she and I can finally persuade Dad to get a pink sofa?!

A ghoul can dream, right?

Smooches,

Draculaura

Start your own fangtastic diary, just like Draculaura! On the following pages, write about your own creepy-cool thoughts, hopes, or screams...whatever you want! These pages are for your eyes only! (Unless you want to share what you write with your ghoulfriends!)

MONSTER HIGH

I hat

Erlow

Did you 💟 reading Draculaura's diary?
Then you will totes love reading
FRANKIE STEIN'S DIARY...
COMING SOON!